Oranges in No Man's Land

Oranges
in No Man's Land

Elizabeth Laird

Haymarket
Books

First published in 2006 by Macmillan Children's Books, London
Text © 2006 Elizabeth Laird
Illustrations © 2006 Gary Blythe

This edition published in 2008 by Haymarket Books
Haymarket Books
P.O. Box 180165, Chicago IL 60618
www.haymarketbooks.org
773-583-7884

This book was publisehd with the generous support of the
Wallace Global Fund.

ISBN 978-1931859-56-1
Library of Congress Data is available

Printed in Canada

To Jehan Helou

Preface

I lived in Beirut during the civil war that raged in
Lebanon thirty years ago. We stayed at first in an
apartment in the ruined center of the city. There
was no furniture. Some of the windows had been
blown in, and lines of bullet holes ran around the
walls of the bare living room. Our six-month-old
son slept in a suitcase on the floor.

Thousands of refugees, fleeing the Israeli inva-
sion of southern Lebanon, had found shelter in sim-
ilar apartments. They crammed in wherever they
could, several families sharing each room.

Later, when we had a place of our own, we
would watch the destruction of the city from our
balcony, hearing the dull crump of the bombs and
seeing billows of smoke rise from the buildings.

I took my son out for a daily walk. The soldiers
on the checkpoints would put their guns down

when they saw him and lift him up in their arms, reaching inside their camouflage fatigues for a piece of candy to put in his hand.

Once, when we were driving home, we realized that the streets were eerily empty. The market had been abandoned. A fruit stall had been knocked over and bright golden oranges were still running down the street. The air crackled with the tension of the battle that was about to start.

It was these and other memories that inspired this book. When I wrote it, I didn't know that Lebanon would plunge back so soon into a nightmare. Caught up in that nightmare are children like Ayesha and Samar, whose lives political leaders so easily throw away.

Elizabeth Laird, 2006

One

I was born in Beirut. It had been a lovely city once, or so Grandma told me. The warm Mediterranean Sea rolled against its sunny beaches, while behind the city rose mountains that were capped with snow in the winter. There were peaceful squares and busy shops and hotels bustling with tourists.

My father and mother were farmers. They came from the countryside south of the city. They'd been happy in their little village. But they lost everything when Lebanon, our country, was invaded. They had to run away to Beirut, the capital. They had three children there: me first, and then my two brothers.

My father built a little house with his own hands in the poorest part of town, where everyone was crowded together in narrow lanes. All our neighbors were like us—refugees from southern Lebanon—trying to manage on nothing, but thankful at least to be safe.

But just after I was born, all that changed. A terrible civil war tore the city of Beirut apart. I pray that those years never come again! I can never forget the horror of them.

And yet, in among all the sad things, the fear and destruction and loss, there are wonderful memories too, of kindness and courage and goodness.

I'll have to start my story, though, with the saddest thing of all.

Ours was a house of women and children, my grandmother, my mother and my little brothers Latif, who was seven, and Ahmed, who was still only a baby. My father was abroad most of the time, looking for work. He'd been gone for so long we were used to him being away. I'd almost begun to forget what he looked like.

When, on that terrible day, the bombs started to fall all around our house, my mother threw some clothes into a bundle and began to pack bags and cases.

"There's no time for that!" Grandma screamed at her, looking out anxiously into the street. "The gunmen are coming! They'll be here any minute. We must take the children and run!"

Mama went on packing. She pushed a big bag into my hands and a smaller one into Latif's. Grandma was already running down the street with Ahmed in her arms.

"Go on, Ayesha," Mama said to me. "Go with Grandma. I'll be right behind you. Wait for me by the mosque on the corner."

And so we ran, Latif and me, racing ahead of Grandma, who was hobbling along behind us with Ahmed in her arms. And a shell fell on our house just as we reached the end of the street, wiping out our little shack of a house and everything in it. I never saw Mama again.

Two

It was a bright morning in Beirut. . . . No, I can't begin there. I must think back a bit further, to the place we found to live in during those muddled, desperate weeks after Mama died. I don't want to remember the first few days, the panic and confusion and the aching, aching loss.

It was Latif who found the apartment for us. Little brothers do have some uses, I suppose, although I didn't often think so then.

The four of us were sitting on a doorstep in a ruined street, feeling hungry and hopeless, after two days of wandering from place to place. All we'd thought about was how best to get away from the fighting. We had no food left and no idea where we'd spend the night. Grandma looked so old and worn and beaten I could hardly bear to look at her. I think she'd given up hope. Ahmed was crying.

"There are people up there, in that window," Latif suddenly said, pointing across the road to the first floor of the building opposite. "Look, Grandma, they're waving to us."

That was the first kind, good thing that had happened to us since the disaster, and it was how we met Samar (who was ten years old like me) and Samar's mother, dear Mrs. Zainab, the best mother in the world, after mine.

A few minutes later we'd crossed the road, pushed open the broken street door of the building, gone up the dusty steps and found ourselves in what must once have been a beautiful apartment where rich people would have lived.

I can remember standing in the doorway looking around in amazement. I'd never been in such a place before. The windows had all been blown out, and there were gaping holes in the walls where shells had blasted through, but you could still see how magnificent it had been in the old days.

Even the hallway was huge. The floors were made of marble, and there were big mirrors on the walls with elaborate gold work around them. You could see beyond the hall into amazing rooms, all light and airy with high ceilings from which ruined chandeliers hung at crazy angles.

The people who had owned this apartment must have left long ago, and they'd taken their beautiful furniture and fancy clothes with them. But the rooms weren't empty. They were full of people. Refugees. Squatters. Poor people from the bombed-out parts of town. People with nowhere to go. People like us.

I could see through the open doors that they'd made corners of the rooms their own. They'd set up little homes, with their own mattresses and cooking pots, and strung up cloths on strings to make partitions so that each family could have a bit of privacy.

Mrs. Zainab came out into the hall toward us. She was comfortable-looking, with smile-wrinkles around her eyes. She wore a long tattered dress and had a scarf tied over her head.

"You poor things," she said. "I couldn't let you go on sitting there, with night coming on and all. Have you got somewhere to go? Are you lost?"

It was then that Grandma burst into tears, and Latif and I were so shocked we huddled up against each other, not knowing what to say. We'd never seen her cry before.

Mrs. Zainab took charge at once. She had found us a corner of our own, in what had been the living room, I suppose. She borrowed a mattress for Grandma, changed Ahmed's diaper and gave us some of her family's supper to share.

And so we bedded down that first strange night in the apartment—Grandma on the mattress, Latif and me curled up on a mat and Ahmed in our old suitcase, which was now his cot.

That was how we found our new home, and that was where we lived, through the freezing cold of winter and the boiling heat of summer, until the old life with Mama in our little shack had begun to seem like a distant dream.

Three

One morning I stepped out of that crowded, overflowing, noisy apartment. It must have been early summer because the night had been cool and the day looked as though it would be hot.

There had been a ferocious gun battle raging in the streets around us all through the night. There was an invisible line across Beirut in those days. It was known as the "Green Line" and it divided the city as surely as a wall, though there was no actual line to be seen, only a vast maze of bombed-out buildings, infested with gunmen and a few old people. The different groups controlled the opposite sides, and the battles were fought across it.

Back then, I never understood who was who or what was what. I still don't really know. What were they all fighting for? Religion? Politics? Was it the rich against the poor? Sometimes I wonder if the fighters themselves knew what they were doing.

That night, they'd been hard at it. The whole city had echoed to the crash of exploding bombs and shells and the rattle of machine-gun fire. Vehicles had roared through the streets, their tires squealing, and ambulance sirens had sounded in the distance.

It was quiet in the streets now. The fighting was over for the time being. The sky should have been a bright blue, but a light fog hung in the air from the dust of the ruins and the smoke from the burning buildings.

There had been so much noise in the night I hadn't slept much, and I was yawning my head off. I hadn't wanted to go out at all, but Grandma had insisted.

"Go down to the checkpoint quickly now," she had said. "I heard the refugee truck's coming today and they're going to give out cooking oil. If you get there early you'll have a better chance of getting some."

"Can't Latif go?" I'd said, frowning at Latif, who'd broken a cardboard packing box open on to the dust-covered floor and was turning somersaults on it.

"No, *habibti*. He'll only get into trouble. Go on now, there's a good girl. The oil bottle's nearly empty. How can I cook? You want to eat, don't you? And take Ahmed with you. He's been pestering to go out since he woke up."

So I'd picked Ahmed up and set off. He was a weight, I can tell you, ten months old and hefty with it. I carried him on my hip, but I kept having to move him from one side to the other.

The street was strewn with rubble, and I was wearing rubber flip-flops, so I had to pick my way carefully to avoid the fresh splashes of broken glass.

I can picture it clearly now, though at the time I hardly noticed the mess all around. There were twisted spikes of metal sticking up from the pavement. They had once been street lights. The gaping dark openings on each side of the road had been busy, crowded shops. The wooden stumps in the middle of the traffic circle were all that remained of palm trees. Their lovely long green fronds had long since been shot away.

All over the asphalt there were circles like you see on the water when you drop a pebble into a pond. They were where shells and mortars had fallen.

The checkpoint wasn't far. I slowed down as I approached it. You had to be very cautious with checkpoints. You had to take care and look closely to make sure that the men guarding them were from a friendly militia. To tell you which militia was running the checkpoint, each one had a little flag stuck up on a pole, or one hanging across the chain that they used to stop the traffic going down the street. Sometimes there were posters too, of the different political leaders. Our flags were green and black.

There were four militiamen there that morning. They had built up two walls of sandbags on either side of the street and had run their chain across between them to stop vehicles going through. They all carried automatic weapons, slung casually over their shoulders. They didn't frighten me though. I knew their flag was the right one for my sort of family. I recognized their accents too. They were the same as mine. They came from the far south of Lebanon. They were Shia Muslims, like us.

Even so, I could never be really relaxed around the militiamen. They had guns, after all, and were very used to using them. I never quite knew what they might do next. Some of them had seen so much fighting and killing I wasn't sure if they knew when to stop.

My heart sank when I came around the corner and saw the checkpoint, because the little truck that usually brought supplies in for refugee families wasn't there. I can remember standing awkwardly, not quite knowing what to do, pushing a stone around with the tip of one rubber sole.

One of the militiamen had taken off his scarf and was retying it around his head. He saw me standing there feeling foolish and beckoned me across. Shyly I went over to him.

"Looking for someone?" he said.

"The truck. My grandma said it was coming today. With cooking oil."

One of the other men heard.

"You'll be lucky. After last night's bombardment? They haven't cleared the roads yet. Tomorrow, *inshallah*. Come back tomorrow."

The light glinted on the gun he was cradling in his arms. Ahmed saw it and reached out to touch it. I snatched his hand back, but the man laughed.

"Hey, little tiger. A fighter already?" He put his gun down on the ground and reached out his arms. "Here. Give him to me."

I didn't want to. How would I know what he might do with a baby in his arms? But Ahmed was struggling and reaching out. He wasn't scared at all. He wanted to pull at the militiaman's headscarf.

"Don't worry, sweetheart. He'll be fine with me." The man had taken Ahmed already and was holding him gently, expertly tickling his tummy. I relaxed a bit. I could see he was used to babies. Ahmed wriggled. He'd gone red in the face and was laughing so hard he was gasping.

"I love him, God save me," the man said. "When

I see him, I see my own son." He seemed quite sorry to hand him back to me. "Come tomorrow and bring him with you. The truck's sure to be here then. You'll get your supplies. And I'll get some extra milk for this one if I can."

So I had to turn back then and go home.

Four

Grandma was cooking when I got back. She was squatting over a small kerosene stove she'd managed to get hold of, stirring a stew of chickpeas.

I never thought about where our food came from. Somehow there always seemed to be something to eat. Now I realize that Grandma must have performed miracles to keep us all fed. There were handouts from the refugee organizations, of course, but they were never really enough. Sometimes she used to leave Ahmed with me and tell me to keep an eye on Latif. Then off she'd go, a determined look on her face, holding one hand to her side to support her painful hip. She'd come back an hour or so later with some fresh vegetables or a little piece of meat, or some cheese wrapped up in a cloth.

"No oil," I said, dumping Ahmed down on the floor and easing my tired shoulders. "The truck wasn't there. The soldiers at the checkpoint said to try again tomorrow."

"You didn't hang about talking to them, I hope," she said with a disapproving frown. Grandma was always fussy about me talking to strangers.

"It's all right, Grandma. They were kind. One of them played with Ahmed."

She pursed her lips, but didn't say anything more.

Ahmed took off at a fast crawl toward the sound of toddlers playing beyond the cloth Mrs. Zainab had hung up for us to give us our own "room." I was about to go and fetch him back, but Grandma gave me a smile, then put up a hand to wipe her forehead.

"Don't worry about him, *habibti*. Mrs. Zainab's there. She'll look after him." She passed me the spoon she'd been using to stir the stew. "Watch this, will you? It'll stick and burn if you're not careful. I must lie down for a minute."

I think that was the first moment when I realized that something was wrong with Grandma. She'd always grumbled about her sore hip, and I'd always known she had to take pills for something or other, but I'd never thought about it much. Why would I? She'd always been there, as far as I was concerned. She'd always looked after us, even when Mama was alive. She would be there forever, or so I'd thought.

Now, for the first time, I saw that she was pale and her face was puffy around the eyes.

"Are you all right, Grandma? Have you taken your medicine?"

"I'm fine. Keep stirring. It only needs a few more minutes."

She limped over to the mattress. It looked quite odd, that bare, dusty old mattress, lying under the remains of what must once have been a beautiful mirror hanging on the wall above, but I'd long since stopped noticing. What worried me now was that Grandma seemed to be shivering, and although it was warm since the chill of morning had worn off, she was covering herself with a blanket.

Five

I haven't told you about Samar yet, and she needs to be properly introduced. To be honest, when I'd met her that first evening, and for days afterwards, I was scared of her. I didn't know what to make of her.

Samar didn't speak. She made grunting, squeaking noises instead, and her hands flew about all the time in complicated, flicking movements.

"It's all right," Mrs. Zainab said, seeing my alarm. "Samar's not stupid. She's deaf, that's all. She can't hear what you say to her, but she can read your lips. Just make sure she can see your mouth when you speak. She'll understand all right."

She must have seen the wary look on my face because she frowned as if I'd annoyed her.

"Samar's missing her friends," she said. "Before all this trouble began, she used to go to the deaf school. Top of the class, she was. They taught her sign language there. None of us can do it properly, and she gets really frustrated when we can't understand. She's lonely. You don't have to be friends with Samar, Ayesha, but she'd love to be friends with you."

I could see she was worried about Samar, and that I might be about to offend her. I didn't know what to do. Then I heard a noise behind me. Samar was there. She'd been reading her mother's lips. Now she was looking at me with her head on one side. She took hold of my hand.

"That means she likes you," Mrs. Zainab said.

I still wasn't sure. I'd never met a deaf person before. I didn't know what to do. But Samar did. She pulled a ball of string out of her pocket, and before I knew what she was doing she'd looped it around my hands.

"She wants to play cat's cradle," said Mrs. Zainab.

"What's that?" I said.

Samar rolled her eyes and grinned at the same time. She looked really funny and sassy. She didn't need sign language to show what she was thinking. What? Never played cat's cradle? Where have you been, you poor, sad girl?

It was so easy to understand her that I burst out laughing. She tugged at my arm. I followed her.

The place she took me to was her special place. It was a quiet corner in a turn of the stair outside the apartment. She showed me the few small treasures she kept hidden behind a loose shutter. There was a little ring with a red glass bead in a matchbox, a yellow plastic rose, and tiny toy teddy bear with a sweet little hat.

That's how I became friends with Samar. She began teaching me her sign language at once. Slowly I began to understand most of what she wanted to say. Anyway, a week later she was as close to me as the sister I never had.

That afternoon, when Grandma went to sleep and

I'd been cooking the chickpeas, Samar poked her head around the screen.

Come on, she signed. Let's play.

So we went to her special place (only it was our special place now). We took out our treasures, hers and mine, and arranged them in a proper order on the windowsill. We always did it the same way, taking a long time over it, before we started to play. It was our little ritual. Once we'd arranged our things, that dusty corner of the ruined stairwell became ours, set apart for us. We never noticed the people who hurried past us to and from the upper floors of the building.

The treasures I'd added to our hoard were a pink butterfly hairgrip that Mama had given me, an embroidered purse that Grandma had stitched and an envelope with a pretty foreign stamp on it, in which Baba had sent a letter to Mama from abroad.

The hours flew by that afternoon, as they always did when we played. I couldn't begin to tell you all that we did. Cat's cradle was only part of it. Samar was the best person I'd ever met at making up games—clever, funny games you could play for hours in the same small space.

Like many other days, we played all afternoon, until the *muezzin* from the mosque nearby sang out the call to evening prayer and I told her it was time to go back in.

When I got back to our corner Latif was nowhere to be seen. Mrs. Zainab was minding Ahmed, and Grandma was still lying down.

"I'm sorry, darling," she murmured. "You'll have to manage the supper by yourself."

So I spooned out the chickpeas and found a few olives and a bit of bread to go with them, and I mashed bits up for Ahmed and fed him with them, and gave some to Latif, who'd come home with a skinned knee and was picking bits of grit out of it.

I took a plate across to the mattress, but Grandma just waved it away.

"Maybe later," she said.

It was dark by now. No one dared go out after dark, no one except for the fighters. People huddled in their corners of that echoing, high-ceilinged apartment and talked, or listened to the news on their radios. That evening, though, we had a few visitors. Friendly faces looked into our corner, one after the other, to ask how Grandma was doing.

"How is she? Better?" they'd say, smiling sympathetically at me. "Wallah, Ayesha, what a good girl you are. A fine mother you'll be one of these days, the way you look after those two brothers of yours."

I don't know why, but their kindness didn't comfort me at all. It frightened me. It made me realize that something was seriously wrong.

Mrs. Zainab was the only one who seemed to know what to do. She brought Grandma some mint tea and knelt beside her, trying to coax her to drink.

"Where's her medicine, Ayesha?" she asked me.

"She keeps it in the box by her pillow."

"Finished. It's finished," Grandma croaked.

I saw Mrs. Zainab's lips tighten, and my stomach lurched. She took Grandma's hand and squeezed it.

"Where did you get your medicine from, Auntie? Can we get some more for you?"

"She brought it with us when we came," I said. "She couldn't afford to buy it. It's really expensive. Dr. Leila gave it to her."

"Dr. Leila?" Mrs. Zainab looked puzzled.

"Yes." My skin was prickling with fear. "Grandma used to work for Dr. Leila. She cleaned her house. Dr. Leila lives downtown. Beyond the *Burj*."

"But that's on the other side of the Green Line!" Mrs. Zainab said, the worry lines deepening on her forehead.

I took a deep breath.

"Will she be all right, Auntie? What if we can't get any more medicine?"

Mrs. Zainab didn't look at me. Her eyes were fixed on Grandma's pale face. Then she said, "It's in the hands of God, *habibti. Inshallah* she will get well."

Six

The rest of the evening passed in a daze. Mrs. Zainab stood up after a while and went out through our curtain. I could hear her talking to some women on the other side, and then came their low murmurs of sympathy.

I sat down beside Grandma. A black hole of nothingness seemed to have opened up in front of me.

"Grandma! You can't die—you mustn't! What am I supposed to do? I can't manage on my own. You know I can't!"

I should have been feeling sad, I suppose, but instead I was angry, and terribly afraid.

Grandma opened one eye and tried to fix it on me, but it wandered away.

"You'll be all right. Big girl. Good girl. Look after . . . Mrs. Zainab—she'll . . ."

"She can't look after us! She's not our family! Please, Grandma, don't die!"

I was calling to her loudly now, my voice breaking up with tears.

Then I felt arms lifting me away. I was hustled through the curtain and two of the old women took their place beside Grandma. Mrs. Zainab fetched Latif and Ahmed and made us lie down to sleep beside Samar when it started to get late.

"Don't worry, don't worry," she kept saying. "God is great. He sees our suffering. If it's his will, he'll spare her. Go to sleep now. You need your strength. Whatever happens, I'm your friend."

Slowly the countless people in that crowded apartment settled down to sleep and soon there was silence, except for a few bursts of coughing and some loud snores, and the quiet murmurs of the two old women who were watching beside Grandma.

I lay with my eyes open, looking up at the distant white ceiling. A terrible loneliness was making me shiver, as if I was being gripped by the chill of winter. But an idea had sprouted in my head, and it was growing clearer all the time.

I've got to do it, I kept telling myself. I've got to find Dr. Leila. It's not far across the Green Line. I could just slip through the ruins and out the other side. Who would want to hurt me, anyway? I'm only a child.

I tried to plot in my mind the route I'd have to take. I'd walked through the old streets of downtown Beirut quite often before the fighting had begun. Mama used to take me on Fridays to visit Grandma at Dr. Leila's house. I'd never noticed the way particularly, but I reckoned I could find it. The roads were quite straight. You just had to go on down the long main road and you'd get to the *Burj*, in the middle of old Beirut.

The invisible Green Line dividing the city ran right through the *Burj*, which was a huge open square. It would be much too dangerous to cross. I'd have to circle around through the streets to the north of it. And once I was beyond the *Burj* I would find my way quite easily.

Several times during that long night I sat up and groped for my flip-flops, steeling myself to set out at once. But then a burst of distant gunfire or the crump of an exploding bomb made me lie down again. It was dangerous enough trying to cross the Green Line in the daytime. It would be total madness at night, when gunmen stalked the streets, armed to the teeth and as jumpy as cats, ready to fire at the slightest sound.

So I lay back down again. I must have slept for a while, but I woke very early and waited and waited for the dawn.

Seven

In the morning Grandma's breathing was shallow and her lips were blue. She didn't stir when I bent over to kiss her. Mrs. Zainab moved me gently away.

"Why don't you and Samar take Ahmed and go down to the checkpoint?" she said. "The supply truck might have come by now. See if they've got oil today."

In the night I'd promised myself that I'd slip off and find my way to Dr. Leila's as soon as I possibly could, but when daylight had come my courage had almost gone.

What if I end up dead too? I'd kept asking myself. Who'd look after my brothers then?

I knew, though, that I had to make myself brave.

"I've got to go to the checkpoint on my own," I tried to tell Samar. "I can't explain. I'll see you later."

Samar looked hurt for a moment, then nodded.

Go, she signed. I'll look after Ahmed.

This is it, I thought. I've got to do it now. And I ran down the stairs and outside.

The air hung heavy in the streets and thick dark clouds were rolling in from the sea. There would be rain soon, I could tell.

The way to the checkpoint seemed endlessly long. I tried to hurry, but I couldn't help slowing down. I could hardly believe that only yesterday I'd been nervous of the men who manned it. They were on our side, keeping us safe. It would be a different matter once I'd slipped past them into the no man's land that lay beyond.

The same soldiers were on duty today.

"Hey, *habibti*, where's that little tiger of yours?" one of them called out to me.

I hadn't expected them to remember me.

"He's sick," I said, trying to think. "Where's the truck? You said it would be here today. Grandma said to get some oil. She needs it. I've got to get oil."

I knew I was babbling on, sounding like an idiot, but my brain was working furiously. Somehow I had to slip past them and get into the dead, dark, ruined city that lay ahead.

I'd been a fool to come to the checkpoint so early. I should have waited till there were people around. As it was, I was the only one out in the streets, apart from the militiamen. There was no one else to distract them.

Just then, when my silly chatter was running down, like a talking toy when the battery starts to die, the first huge drop of rain splashed down on to the shattered pavement, as round and dark as an old coin. The men looked up at the sky, then at each other.

"Here it comes."

"Where did you put the rain ponchos?"

"I left them in the jeep."

"Go and get them then. Think they'll keep us dry, piled up over there? Where are your brains?"

"Get out of here, kid," the nice one said, the one

who had played with Ahmed yesterday. "You'll fall sick like your little tiger if you get soaked through."

I was so used to doing what I was told that I automatically turned around, ready to run obediently back to the apartment, but at that moment there came the rumble of an engine and the refugee truck appeared at the end of a side street, coming toward us, weaving from side to side to avoid the debris and the bomb craters.

The rain was coming down fast now. The men were distracted, waiting for their comrade to run back with their ponchos and keeping an eye on the approaching truck.

This was my chance and I took it. I slipped under the chain and bolted down the deserted street, running into no man's land as fast as my flip-flops would let me.

It was a miracle that I got away with it. A kindly angel must have been looking out for me, guiding my steps and turning the men's heads the other way.

I didn't stop running until I'd reached the bend in the road and knew I was out of sight of the checkpoint. Then I dropped right down to a walk. I didn't mean to. I'd meant to go on running all the way and not stop until I'd reached Dr. Leila's house, but I couldn't help myself. It was as if fear was tangling my legs, slowing me down.

I could hardly believe that these were the same streets that Mama and I had walked down together, so long ago. There had been brightly lit shopfronts then, and pavements crowded with people, and cars and trucks bumper to bumper in endless traffic jams.

There wasn't a soul to be seen now. The shopfronts had all been blown out and their contents looted long ago. The old shops were dark, empty caverns now. Their signs hung drunkenly over the street, twisted and rusting. I could see old neon strip lights hanging broken from the ceilings inside. Piles of rubble choked the pavements. Bullet holes pitted every inch of the stone facades, and the shells that had blasted right through the walls had made holes that looked like the empty eye sockets in dead giants' skulls.

The storm had really burst now. The rain was spouting out of the sky, splashing down the broken sides of the buildings. I was soaked to the skin already. The clouds were so low it was half dark, although it was only morning.

A thin cat shot out suddenly from the building beside me, making me leap with fright. My legs responded on their own. Now I was running again, hardly knowing where I was going.

Mama! Mama! I was saying over and over again in my head. In the long months since my mother's death she had become less and less real to me, but I could almost see her beside me now, urging me on.

It can't be much further, I kept telling myself. This street was never so long. My hand was pressed to the painful stitch in my side.

And then I saw it. Ahead of me, stretched across the road, was a chain suspended between two piles of sandbags. Another checkpoint. And the flags that hung from it were white, with the symbol of a tree in the middle of them. They were the wrong flags. The enemy's flags. I'd run right into trouble.

Eight

For one mad moment I thought the checkpoint was deserted. I thought I could just leap over the chain and fly on. But as I put on a spurt, gathering myself for the jump, three men ran out from the ruined shopfront where they'd been sheltering from the rain. They were unslinging their guns from their shoulders as they came, and pointing them at me.

"You, girl. Stop! Where do you think you're going?"

I tried to stop. I was skidding to a halt on the wet road when my big toe, unprotected by my flip-flop sandals, hit a chunk of concrete that had fallen from a building, and I stumbled. Before I landed on the ground, one of them grabbed my arm, wrenching my shoulder painfully.

"Who the hell are you?" he demanded. "Who sent you here?"

Waves of pain were shooting up my leg from my injured toe and for a few precious moments I could do nothing but screw up my eyes and bite my lip. I suppose it was the pain that saved me. It stopped me opening my mouth and gave me time to listen. And as I did, I heard the men's accents. Their Arabic was different from mine. They were from the north of Lebanon. I was from the south. I only had to say one sentence, one word, and they'd know which side of the divide I was on. They'd know I was an enemy. They'd think I was a spy, and they'd have no mercy on me.

So I just stood there, with my mouth open, staring at them, the rain running down into my eyes.

One of the men was still holding my arm in a painful grip. He shook it.

"What's the matter with you? Are you deaf? Where did you come from? What are you doing here?"

I felt quite sure at that moment that it was Mama who had set that concrete block in my way and made me stub my toe, so that I couldn't speak. I could have sworn, too, that she put the idea of Samar into my head.

Deaf, I thought. Samar. Be like Samar.

So I moved my hands about in the secret sign language that Samar had taught me, and I made the little squeaking, grunting noises she made when she tried to speak.

"She's just an idiot," one of the men said. "Let her go."

Thank you, Samar, I whispered in my mind.

The rain stopped then, as suddenly as it had started, and the sun came out. The men seemed to relax. The one who was holding my arm let go. I was just about to take my chance and bolt again when another one grabbed me.

"Oh no you don't, little bird," he said. "How do

we know you're not a spy, eh? How do we know you're not carrying messages under that dress of yours?"

I saw their looks change. Ugliness was in their eyes.

It was all I could do not to scream out, "No! Leave me alone!" Instead, I grunted furiously, twisting and turning, trying to free myself.

Then, from behind, came an angry voice.

"What are you doing, you animals? Leave the child alone."

The man holding me growled and spun around, loosening his grip. I twisted myself free, and I'd have made a bolt for it then, only one of the other men's guns was still pointing straight at me.

Then I saw the man who had called out. He was old, and nicely dressed, with outdated baggy trousers and a long jacket. On his head he wore a red fez with a black tassel, and he carried an ivory cane in one hand, as if he was setting out to walk down a smart shopping street.

As he came closer I could see that he hadn't shaved for a while, and his clothes looked as if they hadn't been washed for a long time. Even so, he looked as out of place in that war-torn, scary street as an elderly dog in a cage full of lions.

"Are you animals?" he said again. "Persecuting a child. Let her go." You could hear by the way he spoke that he was used to being obeyed.

The militiamen looked uneasy, like schoolboys caught in the act.

"Ya, Abu Boutros," one of them said. "This girl came from the other side. How do we know she's not a spy?"

The old man came right up to me, stepping delicately through the puddles and garbage of the street in his polished brown shoes. He rapped his cane on the ground in front of me, and the cloudy blue eyes were stern in his wrinkled brown face.

"Little girl," he said severely, "where are you from? What are you doing here? Answer me now. The truth."

Samar, I thought again. I copied her exactly, the noises she made and the signs she'd taught me.

"The child's a deaf mute," Abu Boutros said, and he patted me kindly on the shoulder. He turned to glare at the men. "And she's soaked to the skin. Aren't you ashamed? Call yourselves men? What has our Lebanon come to when little deaf girls are threatened by bullies like you?" He waved his stick at me. "Run away, child. Shoo! Go home to your mother."

I made myself stare at him, frowning, for a long moment, pretending that I hadn't understood, then I smiled gratefully and took off, racing on down the street toward the *Burj*, afraid, until I'd turned the corner, that a bullet might come slamming into my back.

Nine

I was so out of breath, once the checkpoint was out of sight, that I had to slow down. The storm had rolled on. I could still hear distant thunder as it moved into the mountains behind the city. Once or twice, as I trotted on down the deserted street, I heard a crash from closer at hand. Was the storm returning? Was a bomb exploding? Or were walls caving in somewhere in the ruins all around me?

The wind was still blowing hard. Even though I'd been hot from running, I was starting to shiver now. I heard a strange noise behind me and looked to see. A gust had whipped up some old blue plastic bags, which were flying through the air like demented birds. Then I saw something big, round and spiky spinning down the street toward me. I gasped with fright, then laughed shakily when I saw that it was only the top of a palm tree, blown clean off its stump by the storm.

I was near the center of old Beirut now. To my left, at the end of the street, I could see down into the vast, open space of the *Burj*.

I stopped for a moment, amazed. In the old days, traffic had crawled nose to tail around the edges of the square, and the paved center had been crowded with people. Now, I knew, there were hidden snipers on the top of every building. No one had dared set foot in the *Burj* for months and months.

There was something even odder though than the silence and emptiness. I screwed up my eyes to look more clearly, unable to believe what I was seeing. Plants were pushing right up through the asphalt—little bushes and baby trees, breaking up the hard surface as easily as if it was loose soil.

That glimpse of the great square, so desolate, made me shiver. I hurried on.

The streets around me were changing. I was leaving the ruins behind. The buildings were still pitted all over with bullet holes, like faces marked with acne, but they weren't burnt out or falling down. Some of them still had glass in their windows. No one was around, but the asphalt had been swept clear of debris, as if traffic sometimes came that way.

And then I heard the strangest thing of all—the sound of horses' hooves, and above that the whooping shouts of boys.

"Come on, you broken old nag!"

"Get on with it, you mother of donkeys! Do you want to win this race or not?"

I dived into a doorway and looked cautiously around a pillar as the first horse appeared from a side street. It was an old creature, with red plumes tossing about on its head. It was harnessed to a little tanker, like the ones that came around our streets, on the other side, selling paraffin for oil lamps and stoves. Latif loved those tankers. He was always running alongside them, trying to pat the horse. A boy was driving this one. He was looking over his shoulder and laughing. And then another racing tanker appeared, with another boy astride it. A second later the two horses with their nodding plumes, the tankers, and the laughing boys had splashed through the puddles and disappeared.

I let out a long breath.

I've made it, I thought. I'm on the other side.

Coming out of no man's land was the strangest thing, like stepping from a darkened room into the light. The distance between the frightening emptiness of the ruins along the Green Line and the bustling everyday world on the other side was no more than a few feet away. I just walked straight from one into the other.

There was life here. Normal life. Market traders were doing business all along the sides of the street. Some stalls were piled with fruit and vegetables. Others were selling china, or clothes, toys or radios. People were walking about, doing their shopping, as if they'd never heard that there was a war on at all.

I wasn't afraid of any gunmen now that ordinary people were all around me. Instead, I had a terrible new fear. I'd been quite sure, when I'd made my plan to cross the Green Line, that I'd be able to find my way easily to Dr. Leila's office. I'd seen it clearly before I started out: the flower seller in his yellow shirt on the corner, the ice-cream parlor at the top of the next street, the film posters on their billboard above the door of the cinema.

I couldn't see any of them. Everything had changed. And the biggest, the worst change of all, was that Mama wasn't there.

I'd never been here on my own before. Mama had always been with me, holding my hand as we crossed through the busy traffic, telling me to hurry.

And when I've found Dr. Leila, I thought, or even if I don't, I've got to go back again through no man's land. On my own.

I suddenly felt so lonely and miserable that I sat down on a step, still wet from the storm, and burst into tears.

Ten

"What's the matter with you?" I looked up. A boy was staring down at me. He was dressed in dusty old black trousers and a crumpled sweatshirt.

"Nothing," I said, before I remembered not to speak.

"Suit yourself. I thought you might like this orange, that's all. To cheer you up. My dad sent me over."

I looked across to where he was pointing. Further down the street, one of the fruit vendors was smiling and waving at me.

"Thanks," I said unwillingly. I couldn't tell from the boy's accent where he was from, but his face was sunburnt and he sounded a bit countrified. There was a chance he wouldn't recognize my accent, if his family wasn't from Beirut either.

I sniffed at the orange. I hadn't eaten any fruit for a while. It smelled wonderful.

"You lost, or what?" the boy said.

"No, I . . ." I stopped, looking up at him again. He seemed friendly, and ordinary. "Well, yes, I am. I'm looking for Dr. Leila, but when I visited her before I was with my mom. I can't remember the way."

"Dr. Leila? Never heard of her," the boy said. "Wait here."

He walked back toward his father's stall, his hands in his pockets, looking as if he wanted me to see how grand and grown-up he was. I watched while his father shook his head and pointed with his chin to the stall next door. The boy disappeared behind it.

The sun had come out at last. Its warmth wrapped me around like kindness, and my dress began to steam. Without realizing what I was doing,

I started to peel the orange. The first taste of its delicious sharp sweetness was wonderful.

It brought back a memory too. The last time I'd eaten an orange had been with Grandma. She'd come back triumphantly to the apartment with a bag full of them. She'd peeled some for Latif and Ahmed and me, and we'd sat sharing them from one chipped enamel plate.

Grandma! I thought. What am I doing sitting here? She might be dead by now! I've got to find Dr. Leila!

I threw away the orange peel and jumped up, forgetting the boy, wanting to run, to explore every side street, to force myself to find her. But before I could move, the boy was back again.

"Where do you think you're going?" he said. "I thought you wanted to find Dr. Leila."

"I do!"

"I've found out where she lives. I'll show you if you like."

I felt so grateful I nearly cried again.

"Which way? Show me quick! I've got to see her now!"

It's amazing how quickly your feelings can change. One moment I was lonely and despairing, and the next I felt proud of myself, sure that everything was going to be all right.

The boy walked fast and I had to trot to keep up with him. I really felt like skipping.

"It's a mess around here, isn't it?" I said. "What happened to that old man on the corner back there, who used to sell flowers?"

"He left. Months ago."

"He was really nice. He used to give a me a flower to hold when I was little."

The boy's footsteps slowed.

"He was one of them. From the south. I hated him. It's all the fault of his lot that the war started."

I bit my lip. I'd opened my big mouth too soon. The boy was looking sideways at me now and frowning.

"How come you didn't stay indoors till it stopped raining? Where do you live, anyway?"

My heart started thudding uncomfortably.

"Couldn't," I said shortly. "Grandma needs her medicine. She sent me."

I was trying now to say as little as possible. The boy didn't seem to have recognized my accent yet.

We were in a narrow side street by now. The boy stopped abruptly and pointed.

"Dr. Leila's office is down there. First turn on the right."

"Thanks," I said quickly. "I know the way now."

I ran off. When I reached the corner I looked back. He was standing still, watching me thoughtfully.

Dr. Leila's office was halfway down the next street. In the old days the door was always open, and people had endlessly gone in and out. The door was firmly shut now.

She's gone! She's left! I thought, panic seizing me.

I stood on tiptoe to reach the knocker and rapped it as loudly as I could, then waited with my fists clenched, hoping desperately that someone would come.

At last I heard slippers shuffling toward the door and a woman's voice called out, "Who is it?"

"I've come to see Dr. Leila," I called back.

"She's not here. Who are you?"

I felt like having a screaming fit. I wanted to lie on the pavement, kick my feet on the ground and yell till I was blue in the face like Ahmed when he had a tantrum.

Instead I pounded on the door with both fists.

"She's got to be there!" I yelled. "She's got to help me! I need her!"

At last I heard a key turning in the lock and the door opened a crack. An old woman stood on the other side. Her head was uncovered and she wore a cotton dress that just covered her knees. She was glaring at me.

"Stop that screaming, you little madam. You'll break the door down. Dr. Leila isn't here. Now go away before I teach you what's what!"

Tears were sprouting from my eyes.

"She is here! She's got to be here!"

And then, through my tears, I saw a tall misty figure appear in a doorway behind the old woman.

"Who is it, Auntie?" Dr. Leila said. "Why, it's only a child. Let her in."

Eleven

I don't remember the next bit very well. I suppose I was a real crybaby, but I just couldn't help it. I was so relieved and worried and happy and miserable, all at the same time, that my crying got worse and worse. I couldn't stop. But at last I found myself sitting on the couch in Dr. Leila's consulting room. She was beside me, patting my knee, and her aunt was hovering disapprovingly by the door.

"Now then," Dr. Leila said, in the kind voice I remembered so well, "wipe your eyes, *habibti*, and tell me what's the matter."

I made a huge effort, swallowed hard, blew my nose on the tissue she'd offered me and tried to smile at her. Before I could speak, she lifted my chin with one finger and looked at me with a puzzled frown.

"But I know you, don't I?" she said.

I nodded.

"I'm Ayesha. My grandmother used to work for you."

Dr. Leila's aunt gave a loud sniff. Dr. Leila turned to her.

"I think you're right, Auntie. I can smell it too. Something seems to be burning in the kitchen."

To my relief, her aunt shuffled off.

"So," Dr. Leila said, putting her arm around my shoulders and squeezing gently, "why have you come to see me? Where are you living now? Your grandmother left without a word. She just didn't turn up to work one day. It was after a big bombardment. I was afraid something bad had happened."

I told her all about everything then: the bomb that had killed Mama, and how Grandma had made us run away, and where we'd ended up, in the big old apartment, with lots of other refugees.

"But how did you get here today?" Dr. Leila said. "You must have crossed the Green Line."

"I did. I ran. I nearly got caught by the militiamen. I was really, really scared. An old man saved me from them."

"An old man? In no man's land?"

"He was wearing a fez and he had a cane. He looked—I don't know—funny, being there."

She nodded.

"It must have been Abu Boutros. He's quite famous. He refuses to leave his old home even though it's bombed out and there's no water or electricity."

She was so kind, and the feel of her arm around my shoulders was so comforting, that I knew she wouldn't think I was being silly, and I said, "I thought it was Mama, really, looking after me. I suppose that's stupid. I just felt it."

"Not stupid at all," Dr. Leila said briskly. "But now, tell me, Ayesha, why did you take such a terrible risk to find me?"

So I told her about Grandma, and how sick she was, and how her medicine had run out. She asked me a lot of questions about the way Grandma looked, and where her pain was. I could answer some of them, but not all.

I felt ashamed. I'd never thought about how Grandma felt, or taken much notice when she'd groaned with pain.

"She needs to see a doctor urgently," Dr. Leila said at last, looking worried. "Surely there are still doctors over there, on the other side?"

"We don't know any. We don't have any money to pay," I muttered, my confidence sinking again. "I thought you—I mean, I was hoping . . ."

"Of course I'll help." Dr. Leila had opened a drawer in a filing cabinet and was looking through it. "Good. I kept her notes." She pulled a file out and leafed through it. "When did I last examine her?" She was talking to herself. "Ah yes, the date's here. Blood pressure . . . diagnosis . . . treatment . . ." She looked up at me again. "And the medicines have only just run out, you said?"

I nodded. The worried look was still on her face and it was making me feel awful.

"Please, Dr. Leila, will she die? Is she going to be

all right? I don't think I can manage Latif and Ahmed on my own. Latif never does what I tell him and I don't know how to look after Ahmed, not like Grandma does."

"We're all going to die, Ayesha. It's in God's hands. But I think—very probably—that you've saved your grandmother's life. She's extremely sick though. Looking at these notes I can see that the medicines I gave her should have run out weeks ago. She must have been using only small doses to make them last."

She had taken out a set of keys and was opening the big storeroom that led off her consulting room. I could her murmuring long medical words, but I didn't understand them.

She came out a few moments later with several boxes in her hands.

"I think your mama is still looking after us, *habibti*." I loved the way she said "us." "I was afraid I hadn't got the right stuff. I'm running all my supplies down. But there's most of what your grandmother needs here, enough to keep her going for nearly a year."

I looked at the life-saving boxes in her hands. There seemed to be an awful lot of them.

"We—I—like I said, we haven't got any money," I blurted out. "Are they very expensive?"

"You don't have to pay a thing." She had put the medicine down on the desk and was checking it over. "I owe your grandmother a month's wages at least, and besides, I'm fond of her. Every time I think of her I remember the good days. It didn't matter then that she was from one side and I was from the other. There weren't any sides in the good old days."

She stopped. Her aunt had come back into the room with a cup of coffee on a tray. She put it down sharply on the table so that a bit of it spilled, and she shot an angry look at me.

"There's work to do upstairs, you know," she said to Dr. Leila. "I can't do all the packing myself. I thought you said you weren't taking on any more of your hard cases?"

"Ayesha's not a hard case. She's an old friend. I'll be up in a minute, Auntie." She winked at me as her aunt left the room again.

"Packing? Are you leaving?" I stared at her. Shocked.

"I'm afraid so. I'm going to France. I'll come back when this horrible war's over. But don't worry. Your grandmother's going to be all right. I'll write a note in case you have to try to find another doctor, but I don't think you will. In a year's time, surely, all this will be over, and I'll be home again, and your grandmother will be back in her old job." She had packed the medicine in a bag and was about to hand it to me when she frowned. "Oh dear. There's still one big problem we've got to solve: we have to get you safely home again. Now how, I wonder, are we going to manage that?"

Twelve

I realize now how much trouble Dr. Leila took for me and my grandmother that day. At the time I didn't think of it. I was only aware of a huge sense of relief. I'd done my bit. It was up to the adults now to solve all the problems.

I let myself relax. It was lovely to be sitting on soft upholstery in a clean, quiet room. I hadn't been in a place like that for a long time. It was all so different from our crowded, noisy, dusty apartment, where it was impossible ever to wash properly, or keep the place clean. I leaned back against the cushions of the sofa and looked around at everything, enjoying the lovely smell of Dr. Leila's perfume and gazing at the picture of a lady in a blue robe on the wall and the red flowers growing on the windowsill.

Meanwhile, Dr. Leila was busy on the phone.

"Abu Bashir, please, I'm asking you—yes, and we'll need an ambulance—no, it has to be a United Nations one—Well yes, I'm afraid so—to the other side—Why? Because I have a child here with urgent medicine for her grandmother, and only an ambulance will get through—yes, literally, a matter of life and death—Of course I'm going with you. Would I ask you otherwise?"

I could hear a man's voice talking on and on, making excuses. At last he stopped. Dr. Leila cleared her throat and looked uncomfortable.

"How is your little girl now, Abu Bashir? Did the treatment I gave her work?—Good. That's excellent." There was silence. Then the man said something softly. Dr. Leila's face broke into a smile. "Thank you. So much. I knew I could rely on you. I won't forget this. If it wasn't a very special case I wouldn't have asked you, believe me."

She put the phone down and turned to me.

"You're going home in style, Ayesha, in a UN ambulance, under the blue flag. Now let's go to the kitchen and see what Auntie's been cooking. It'll be at least an hour before Abu Bashir gets here."

Not even the sour looks of Dr. Leila's aunt could spoil that lovely meal for me. There was lamb stewed with okra, and fresh bread, and thick creamy yoghurt, and rice with pine nuts. I'd never eaten anything so good in my life. I put all my worries aside and—I admit it—ate till I was bursting.

In the middle of the meal, Dr. Leila went away to answer the telephone. Her aunt leaned across the table and hissed at me, "Go on, stuff yourself, you little Shia beggar. Go back and tell all your murderous cousins over there how kind and nice we are to scum like you."

And I hate you too, I wanted to say, but I didn't of course. I just went on eating. A moment later Dr.

Leila was back, and five minutes after that there was a loud knock on the door. Abu Bashir and the ambulance had arrived.

I got up to leave.

"Wash your hands before you touch anything," Dr. Leila's aunt scolded. "Think I want to spend all day cleaning up after you?"

I quickly washed my hands at the sink in the corner of the kitchen, and I was glad I had because the soap was lovely, soft and scented, not at all like the hard, rough stuff that was all we could ever afford. Secretly I rubbed it on the front of my dress so that Samar could smell it when I got home.

Abu Bashir was quite big and solid-looking. Little grey curls grew out around the sides of his bald head. He was arguing with Dr. Leila.

"Out of the question, doctor. You're not coming with me. I can't let you put yourself in danger. Not after what you did for my little Lamis. Anyway, you told me last week your UN pass has run out. They'd take you off at the first checkpoint, and I wouldn't be able to do a thing about it."

He saw me sidling around from behind Dr. Leila

with the huge bag of medicines in my hand.

"So this little lady is what all the fuss is about? Come on then, *ya qalbi*. If we're going to do this, we'd better do it now. There's a storm brewing up this afternoon and I don't mean the kind that brings rain."

The ambulance stood just opposite the door. It was sparkly white, with big black letters painted on the side. They weren't Arabic letters, but I'd seen them often enough to know what they meant. UN. United Nations. Protection. The blue UN flag was pinned to a little flagpole on the roof.

I turned around and threw my arms around Dr. Leila's waist. I didn't want to leave her. I wanted to stay forever and ever, bask in her kindness, listen to her soft voice, and feel her arm around my shoulders. And, to be quite truthful, I wanted to go on eating her lovely food and using her lovely soap. In spite of her nasty aunt, at that moment I'd quite forgotten that she was on one side in the war that had killed my mother, and I was on the other.

"Go on, *habibti*," she said, lifting me up to kiss me as if I was a small child. You're the bravest girl

I've ever met, and that's saying something, I can tell you."

As I ran to the ambulance, she called something after me, then went back inside her house.

"Did you get that?" Abu Bashir asked me.

"No."

"She said, "Don't grow up to hate anybody." Remember that."

Thirteen

I had expected to ride in the front seat of the ambulance beside Abu Bashir, but instead he opened the back and told me to hop in. Then he took a bandage out of a box and tied it around my head.

"Lie down on the bed," he said. "When we get to a checkpoint you'll have to pretend you're wounded. I'm taking you to see a specialist who lives on the other side, OK? And don't open your mouth. That accent of yours would give you away to anyone."

I nodded and eased the bandage a bit, where it was too tight over my ears. This was going to be dangerous, I knew. My skin was prickling with fright again.

We set off. The ambulance windows were darkened so I knew no one could see me unless they leaned right inside Abu Bashir's window. I sat up and looked out through the black glass.

Something was different. For a moment, I couldn't work out what it was. Then I realized that everything was strangely quiet. There wasn't a soul anywhere.

Abu Bashir was cursing under his breath.

"This is bad. Bad," I heard him say.

I felt shy of Abu Bashir, but I plucked up courage and said, "What's bad, Uncle?"

"The battle. It's going to start." He was hunched over the steering wheel. "The shooting's going to begin any minute now. Hang on, *habibti*. We'll have to make a dash for it."

The ambulance leaped forward with a sudden thrust of speed. I was thrown back, but I clung on to the straps hanging over the bed. We were racing furiously down the street now.

I couldn't believe my eyes. A couple of hours earlier the street had been crowded with people. Now there was nobody. No one at all. The market stalls were still there, left just as they had been, the goods displayed, open and unguarded. The vendors must have sensed what was about to happen and had fled.

Their stuff was safe from thieves though. No one would dare creep out to take it now that the snipers were in position on the upper floors of the buildings.

And it had all happened only moments ago, I could tell, because in their hurry to get away someone had knocked over a fruit stall. It was the very one whose owner's son had shown me the way to Dr. Leila's house. His oranges were still rolling down the street, making a bright stripe of moving color on the black asphalt.

I was used to danger. I'd heard countless bombs exploding, and I'd often gone to sleep to the sound of gunfire. But nothing had ever frightened me as much as that wild dash along the empty street. The world seemed to stand still, holding its breath, waiting for the men of death to open fire.

And they did. Just as we reached the end of the street and plunged through one of the narrow openings into a ruined side alley, the first rattle of machine-gun fire burst out behind us, and the hateful crump of an exploding mortar bomb echoed from building to building.

Fourteen

I'll never forget that mad ride across the Green Line. As the UN ambulance bounced over ruts and rubble, I had to cling on to whatever I could reach, like a monkey in a storm-tossed tree.

The shooting and explosions seemed to go on forever, but in fact we left the battle behind us very quickly and plunged back into no man's land. The ruined streets were as eerily deserted as they had been that morning. Then the distance I'd run had seemed endless, but in the ambulance we covered it in a few minutes. We reached the hostile check-point, the place I'd been dreading most, all too soon. My heart was pounding as Abu Bashir slammed on the brakes and let down his window.

I'd already lain down on the bed, covered myself with the blanket that had been folded on the end of it and turned my face to the side, hoping that if the militiamen looked in they wouldn't recognize me.

I couldn't hear their questions, only Abu Bashir's replies.

"Little girl—head injuries. Yes, I know. Crazy to take her across, but there's some expert over that side—only person—Who? Dr. Leila. Yes, that's right. You know her? She's a true saint, that woman." I sensed him leaning further out of the window. "Wait a minute. Aren't you Ramzi's little brother? Hey! Nice to see you!—The fighting? It's north of the *Burj*. We only just got through—Thanks, boys. Look out for me. I'll drop the patient off and be back as quick as I can."

The window hissed up again. The ambulance moved off. We were through.

I looked at the back of Abu Bashir's head.

He knows those bad men, I thought. They're his

friends. I was worried now. What if Abu Bashir wasn't kind after all?

But he's got a daughter, I thought. He can't be all bad.

I took a deep breath.

"Please, Uncle, how old's your little girl?"

"Lamis? She's ten. Must be around the same age as you, *habibti*. One day, God willing, you might be friends, when all this is over."

So he is nice after all?

It was too confusing. I didn't know what to think anymore.

We turned a corner. In the distance I could see the next checkpoint, but this was the one I knew well, where the kind militiamen, the ones on our side, had played with Ahmed.

"We've made it!" I burst out happily. "Look! They'll let us through all right. I know them. I'm nearly home. We're safe now."

But the ambulance had slowed right down to a halt.

"You may be safe," Abu Bashir said, running a hand across his bald head. "I'm not so sure about me. Did you say you knew those guys?"

"Yes! They're nice. They offered to get some milk for my little brother."

"Did they now? And your home, it's not far from here?"

"Only a little way. You have to turn right at the traffic lights (only they're not working now), and on past the shoe shop on the corner. I'll show you."

"I'd rather you didn't, *habibti*. As a matter of fact, I'd rather not go any further. If I let you out here, will you be all right on your own? You're sure you know the way?"

He sounded worried.

"You don't need to be scared of them, Uncle," I said. "Honestly. They're really kind."

But he was already turning the ambulance around.

"Kind to you, maybe. Look, I'll wait here and watch to see that you get through all right. Can you manage that door alone? Good. Got the medicines?" He was leaning out of the driver's window. He put out a hand and pinched my cheek.

"You're a good girl, Ayesha. A great little girl.

I'll tell Lamis all about you. And say hello to your grandmother for me. I hope she gets better soon."

"Don't drive back there," I said. "What about the fighting? You'll run straight into it. You might get shot."

"I'll be all right. I'll wait for a lull. Those boys back there will look after me. Off you go now. Wait! Take the bandage off your head. If your grandmother sees you wearing that, the shock might be too much for her."

Fifteen

I unwound the bandage and gave it back to Abu Bashir. I tried to thank him, but the words wouldn't come properly. I could think of only one person now. Grandma. I realized that I'd hardly given her a thought during these last packed hours, but now all my worries came surging back.

She might have died already! I might be too late!

I was almost at the checkpoint before the men guarding it saw me. They shouted to each other and swivelled their guns in my direction. With a shock I saw that they now looked just as frightening as the men at the enemy checkpoint. They were glaring at me with the same expression in their eyes.

"Stop! Who are you! Where are you going?"

They hadn't recognized me.

"It's me," I said. "The little tiger's sister."

They lowered their guns.

"What do you think you're doing?" one of them said sternly. "You know you mustn't pass the checkpoint without telling us. It's dangerous over there. What's in that bag?"

I thought quickly. I didn't want to tell them I'd been right into enemy territory.

I hung my head and pretended to look foolish and ashamed.

"I—Grandma sent me to look for something to light the fire. Our paraffin's run out. I thought—I was looking for pieces of wood. I only found some old cardboard boxes."

For a moment, I thought they were going to search my bag, but a car coming from the other direction distracted them.

"Don't sneak past us again, you silly kid. Go on. Get lost."

I darted away from them, racing for home, the bag of medicines bouncing against my leg.

When I reached the familiar entrance to the old stairwell I nearly fell over Samar, who was sitting on the bottom step, her arms around her knees. Tears had made dark tracks down the dust on her cheeks.

My heart almost stopped when I saw the woeful look on her face.

"Grandma!' I shouted. "She's not . . ."

Samar shook her head. She stood up. She was trying to tell me something urgently, her strange noises louder than usual, and her hands flying about too fast for me to follow.

She stopped trying at last and signed a question.

Where have you been?

I pointed east.

"To the other side. To Grandma's doctor. See?"

She looked inside the bag, grinned with delight and nodded furiously.

I knew. I knew where you'd gone. I told them you were out looking for food, to stop them worrying.

It was only afterwards that I learned what she'd been trying to tell me. I was too impatient just then to stop and work it out. I pulled her toward the stairs, but she shook me off. I flew up them to our floor, and then I was once more in the apartment, crossing the marble-floored hallway, running to our corner and lifting up our curtain.

Sixteen

Grandma's eyes were shut and her face was a horrible gray color. For one dreadful moment I thought I'd come too late. There was a woman sitting on the floor beside her, fanning her gently with a corner of the cloth, but it wasn't Mrs. Zainab. It was someone from another room in the apartment.

"Grandma!' I called out too loudly.

The woman frowned and put a finger to her lips.

"Shh. She's sleeping."

I didn't take any notice. I dropped to my knees beside Grandma's dusty old mattress.

"Grandma, I've got your medicines. I've got them here. I went to see Dr. Leila. Look."

I upended the bag and tipped the cartons of medicines out on to the mat.

Grandma opened her eyes and looked at me, but I couldn't tell if she'd understood me or not. Her gaze held mine for a moment, then wandered, and her eyes closed again.

The woman put out one hand from under the black chador that covered her from head to toe and picked up one of the medicine cartons.

"You've seen a doctor? Is this stuff good for coughs? Can I have some for my daughter?"

I hardly heard her. I'd opened Dr. Leila's letter and was trying to read it, but I couldn't make anything of her scrawly writing.

"I don't know what to do!' I wailed, suddenly feeling helpless. "I don't know what to give her!'

The curtain moved and Mrs. Zainab came in with Ahmed balanced on her hip. He saw me and squealed with joy, putting out his arms.

"Ayesha! Wherever have you been?" She looked annoyed. "Fancy disappearing like that, today of all days, with your grandmother so sick. Especially with this news that's come through. I've got so much to do, I . . ."

I wasn't listening. I held up Dr. Leila's letter.

"Please, Mrs. Zainab, what does it say? Dr. Leila's written down what to give her, but I can't read it."

"Dr. Leila? What are you talking about?"

She was looking at me, not at the letter. I was so impatient I wanted to scream.

"I went to see her," I said, all in a rush. "I ran. Across the Green Line. I found her. She gave me all this stuff for Grandma. A UN ambulance brought me back."

Her mouth was open. She was staring at me.

"You . . . ? But Samar said you'd gone off to look for food. You mean you went all the way across no man's land? Alone?"

"Yes, but quick, Mrs. Zainab, please read the letter. I want to give Grandma her medicine now."

While we'd been speaking, the other woman had got up and slipped away. I could hear her high, cracked voice behind the curtain, telling anyone in the apartment who would listen what that little wonder Ayesha had done.

I hardly heard. My eyes were fixed on Mrs. Zainab's face. She was reading the letter slowly, her lips moving. Then she bent down, picked up one of the boxes and opened it.

"Get some water, Ayesha," she said crisply.

By the time I was back with a glass of water, she was kneeling on the mat, her arm under Grandma's head, which she was carefully lifting.

"Come on, Auntie," she said. "Swallow it down. And a sip of water."

Grandma's hand, waxy pale, feebly held the glass, then fell back on to the blanket again. But her eyes were wide open. She was looking at me, and I saw that she'd understood everything.

Her lips moved.

"What did she say?" I'd leaned forward too late.

"*Allah u akbar,*" Mrs. Zainab said. "God is great."

Grandma didn't say any more, but her hands

reached up toward me. I bent over her, ready to listen in case she tried to speak again. Instead she took my face between her two hard palms, drew my head down, and kissed me on the forehead with trembling lips.

Seventeen

Grandma started looking better almost straight away. I don't think, looking back, that the medicine could have worked at once. But I think she'd started to feel hopeful. She'd almost given up before I'd come home, and was waiting to die. Now, she knew she had a good chance to live, and she was determined to take it.

I felt like a film star for the next few hours. People kept coming into our corner to praise me and ask me questions.

"*Wallah*, Ayesha, you're a dark horse. Who'd have thought a little thing like you. . ."

"What's it like over there, Ayesha? Did you look into the *Burj*? Is it still completely empty? Is the cinema still there?"

"Why didn't you tell me you were going to get medicines for free? My eyedrops ran out weeks ago."

"I hope they're suffering over there, same as we are over here."

Ahmed wasn't impressed, of course. He'd whined for something to eat as soon as he'd seen me. But Latif crept in after a while and sat cross-legged on the other end of the mat, staring at me with open eyes.

When everyone had gone he said, "Are you really a heroine, Ayesha? Did anyone shoot at you? Why didn't you let me go? I'd have been a heroine too."

"No, you wouldn't. Only girls can be heroines."

He scowled.

"That's not true. I'm just as brave as you are."

"Boys can be heroes. Girls are heroines."

I realized, as I watched him think about this, that I hadn't properly looked at my little brother for a long time. I saw how thin he was and how dirty.

"Grandma's going to get better," I said. "She's not going to die."

His brows flew up.

"What do you mean? She wasn't going to die anyway, was she? You never said. You're making that up, aren't you?"

"I'm not. But she won't, now I've got her medicine."

He shivered.

"If you're wrong, and she does, who's going to look after us till Daddy comes and finds us?"

"We'd have to look after ourselves. We'll have to anyway. She probably won't be really better for ages."

His eyes were enormous.

"I can't look after us."

I saw my opportunity and I seized it.

"Yes, you can. You can come when I call you, and mind Ahmed when I ask you to, so that I can do the cooking and stuff." I thought of something else. "And you can go to the checkpoint and get our supplies when the refugee truck comes. You can be in charge of that."

I'd had enough of armed men and checkpoints. I never wanted to go near them again.

He nodded, looking serious and grown up.

"We'll manage," I said. "Mrs. Zainab will help us."

What he said next made me open my eyes in horror.

"No, she won't. They're leaving. Tomorrow. Didn't Samar tell you?"

Eighteen

I don't know how long I sat there staring at Latif. I do remember saying, "No. No! It's not true. You're just saying it. How do you know, anyway?"

Latif shrugged. His moment of seriousness was over. He wasn't interested in Mrs. Zainab and Samar.

"Ask them," he said. "I wasn't listening properly. Can I go and play now?"

It was the first time he'd ever asked my permission for anything. In spite of my shock, I was impressed. I nodded, feeling important.

"Yes, but come back soon. It'll be dark in an hour."

I stood up when he'd gone. I looked at Grandma, but she'd turned on to her back and was asleep, her mouth open. I realized for the first time that it had been at least two hours since I'd seen Samar. I was angry.

Why didn't she tell me they were going? I thought. Doesn't she care about me at all?

Then I remembered how Samar had been crying on the step, and how frantically she'd tried to talk to me. I lifted the curtain and slipped out.

Samar was sitting patiently on the floor just outside. I could tell she was waiting for me. In her family's corner I could see Mrs. Zainab packing things away into some big checkered zip-up bags. Already the area looked half deserted.

Mrs. Zainab saw me and came over.

"Don't look so miserable, you two. Here, I'll take Ahmed. Go along on your own for a bit. Just for an hour, mind. And there'll be enough in the pot tonight, Ayesha, for you and the boys."

Samar and I looked at each other and nodded.

A moment later we were in our special place, on the stairs.

We said nothing until we'd unpacked our treasures and laid them out properly on the windowsill. Then we huddled together on the lowest step, not noticing the people who went past us. Slowly we puzzled out each other's stories.

I'd never before felt such a need to understand Samar. Although she'd taught me many of her signs over the past few months, there weren't enough for that special conversation. I could see in her eyes, too, how desperately she was trying to understand me.

But I'll never have an audience like Samar again. For her, I acted it all out—the scary ruins, the horrible men at the checkpoint, old Abu Boutros with his ivory-topped cane, the racing paraffin tankers, the vast emptiness of the *Burj*, the orange seller's boy, Dr. Leila, her nasty aunt, and the mad ride home in the UN ambulance. She laughed, and gasped, and held her breath, and she sniffed at the lingering scent of soap on my dress with delight, putting back her head to hold the smell in her nostrils.

And bit by bit I pieced together her story. It was

simple. Her uncle had come that morning. He had found an apartment just for them. They would be leaving early tomorrow. They would have two rooms, running water, electricity, and windows with glass. And Samar would be going to a new school—a boarding school this time. A special one for deaf children. Her uniform would be blue.

The hour passed quickly. It was dark now. We knew we had to go back in. We stood at the windowsill to reclaim our little treasures, but before I'd even touched them, Samar had swept them all into the box and handed it to me.

I still have those funny things: the ring with the red glass bead, the plastic yellow rose, and the tiny teddy with its dented, faded hat.

I never saw Samar again. Just as the war had brought us together, it brutally divided us once more.

Grandma slowly grew well again over the next few months, and then, one stifling summer day, my father came. He'd searched for us for weeks throughout the city, and he swept us off to an apartment of our own. Our life began again. Slowly, carefully, we put down new roots, afraid at first that they'd be torn up.

Peace returned to Lebanon. Latif went back to school and so did I. Ahmed learned to walk and talk. We all went on growing up.

I often remember that dusty, ruined apartment in old Beirut. And I know that a little part of me will stay there forever, laying out those treasures on the windowsill and playing cat's cradle with my friend.

A Little Piece of Ground

Elizabeth Laird
with Sonia Nimr

Twelve-year-old Karim Aboudi and his family are trapped in their Ramallah home by a strict curfew. In response to a Palestinian suicide bombing, the Israeli military subjects the West Bank town to a virtual siege. Meanwhile, Karim, stuck at home with his teenage brother and fearful parents, longs to play soccer with his friends. When the curfew ends, he and his friend discover an unused patch of ground that's the perfect site for a soccer field. Nearby, an old car hidden intact under a bulldozed building makes a brilliant den. But in this city, there's constant danger, even for schoolchildren. And when Israeli soldiers find Karim outside during the next curfew, it seems impossible that he will survive.

"A fine book, and a daring book."
—Michael Morpurgo, Britain's Children's Laureate

 **Haymarket**Books

Order online at www.haymarketbooks.org or by calling 773-583-7884. Booksellers call Consortium Book Sales and Distribution at 1-800-283-3572.